I0537816

The Christmas Clock and the Magical Elves

Copyright 18/08/2025 by Anita Kirk

All rights reserved. No part of this publication may be reproduced, distributed, or transmitted in any form or by any means, including.

photocopying, recording, or other electronic or mechanical methods, without the prior written permission of the publisher, except in the case of a brief quotations embodied in critical reviews and certain other non-commercial uses permitted by copyright law. This is a work of fiction. Names, characters, businesses, places, and incidents are either the products of the author's imagination or used in a fictitious manner. Any resemblance to actual persons, living or dead, or actual events is purely coincidental.

Dedication

Anita's most popular fan would be
her father before he sadly got
dementia, and he is now
devastatingly blowing in the wind.
Anita's family has supported her
one hundred percent with her
writing, and she thanks them for
the encouragement and you for
taking the time out of your day to
pick her book up and read it.
If you do enjoy reading this book,
Anita would really appreciate a
good review to show other people
that you have enjoyed reading.

Acknowledgments

I would like to thank you for taking the time to pick this book out from the millions of books available out there to read, if you do enjoy reading this book your review would mean the world to Anita Kirk for her to enjoy reading and sharing this book with others on social media or in person would be most appreciated.

Thank you.

Prologue

The elves and Father
Christmas start to panic in
Father Christmas's workshop
in the North Pole when a red
button starts to flash, pointing
out that there is danger
happening worldwide and in
the North Pole with power
outages and Father

Christmas's sleigh does not have enough Christmas spirit to fly.

The Christmas clock has slowed down. Why?

Father Christmas has a little bit of a hiccup before Christmas with magic protected by a force field.

Some magic gets stolen from the Shoe Magic shop

and from people's feet where Father Christmas's elf Isla only lets victims of low Christmas spirit in and controls the force field with a magic gold key.

Does Don the magic stealer stop Christmas from happening by putting a spell on people and draining all of the magic available into their yellow badges from items full of magic dust?

Do Father Christmas's assistants, Poppy, and Karen, find Dom and lock him back up in the secure glasshouse in Leeds?

Dom and Mateo, the magic stealers, hide in different random, strange places.

The Ho, Ho, Ho phone is vital to keep in touch.

Does the Easter Bunny
help to save Christmas?

Do all of the magical
shoes get stolen?

Do all of the five
Christmas sleigh lights work
in time to make sure that all
of the Christmas presents get
where they need to go?

You will have to read this short story full of jokes and funny comments to find out.

Wakefield and Leeds in the United Kingdom are real places.

The Christmas Clock and the Magical Elves

Chapter One

The North Pole

In the North Pole, Father Christmas spoke to one of his

head elf assistants that was smartly dressed in red and green with ears that are slightly pointed on top, and her name is Daisy. "It is the fifth of November, and I have heard Chinese whispers from people in the rest of the wide beautiful world that Dom, the magic stealer, is unfortunately hovering near to Wakefield again!"

Daisy pointed at the Christmas clock on the bright red wall. "The silver twinkling and sparkling Christmas clock is connected to the Magic Shop in Wakefield, West Yorkshire, in the United Kingdom, and it is showing that it is losing time with red writing saying low Christmas spirit on it!"

Father Christmas looked at the Christmas clock. "I have decided that we will leave it a few weeks and see if the clock corrects itself!"

Daisy agreed. "I think that we should be doing something really, but I am not sure what!"

Weeks later.

Father Christmas sounded upset. "What do we do now, because by the look of it, the Christmas clock has clearly not sorted itself out because it is losing time even more, and my grotto is in the process of being set up in every area of the world?"

Daisy shook her head from side to side. "I am sure we can sort this out; Dom was the main reason that we had to introduce the Shoe Magic shop that has got a force field around it to keep Dom out in the first place!"

Father Christmas sounded disappointed. "Dom stole all of the Christmas spirit from the world a few years ago!"

Daisy shook her head side to side. "How?"

Father Christmas stroked his beard. "By sucking it inside of his Christmas reducer machine to benefit himself by using the magic to travel faster through different routes to steal his magical badge back that he has invented!"

Daisy looked shocked. "That's awful!"

Father Christmas blinked heavily. "Dom also increased his power to take over Christmas Eve and give out a lump of coal instead of gifts to every child in the world because of his evil streak!"

Daisy looked puzzled. "Dom invented the Christmas reducer machine as well as the magical badge, is this correct?"

Father Christmas sounded down. "Yes, Dom made them both, and when Dom put a spell on people, stealing their Christmas spirit, it made me feel devastated because all of our five white sparkling power lights on the sleigh had gone out with the result of his actions!"

Daisy exhaled. "I just hope that Dom does not cause trouble again, and did you hear the joke about the aeroplane? It is way over your head!"

Father Christmas sipped his hot cocoa, nearly choking with a laugh. "I know, our magical dust that is on the inside of our shoes may be in danger that we send down to Wakefield into the secret Shoe Magic shop again if Isla let's the wrong people into the Shoe Magic shop in Wakefield by accident!"

Daisy pondered. "I don't know how we can prove that Dom is the culprit, trying to destroy Christmas was a terrible move that landed him in the secure glasshouse, far away from the Shoe Magic shop and that snowman outside of the window looks cute and cosy wearing its ice cap!"

Father Christmas panicked. "I hope that Dom has not got hold of any phones, power banks, magical badges, or cameras where he can store our magic again for his own benefit, connecting it to a badge of some sort and that green and black outfit that Dom wears is frightening!"

Daisy pointed at the silver Christmas clock while looking at her watch on her arm. "I think that the Christmas clock is losing time again like it did when Dom stole the magic before!"

Father Christmas glanced at the silver clock and then Daisy's gold watch on her arm, speaking. "Yes, you are right, this is more serious than I thought, and I have noticed that a snowman waits for the warmer weather to lose weight. I bet most people wish that they could do that!"

Daisy tapped her fingers on the table. "All we can do is hope that Dom has not stolen the dust and yes, if snowmen move to the tropics, they are a puddle!"

The red Ho, Ho, Ho phone rang with Father Christmas

answering. "Hello, are you setting up all of my grottoes all over the world okay, with no problems, ready for me to visit all of our lovely children on our nice list and some on our naughty list in case they change to the nice list?"

The elf answered on the other side of the red Ho, Ho, Ho phone. "I think that we are in trouble because all of our grottoes are vanishing like they have never existed. Someone is taking control of our magic somehow!"

Father Christmas scratched his face. "This has never happened before. How can this happen? I think we need to stay at the North Pole and try to work out our next plan of action!"

The elf could not believe his eyes. "I will ask all our elves to give up attempting to set up our grotto's for now and return to the North Pole using our unique, special, precious magic dust!"

Father Christmas and the elf then put the red Ho, Ho, Ho phone down.

Father Christmas noticed a piece of paper stuck down the crack on the fluffy white seat that he was sitting on with him pulling it out. "What is in this envelope, I wonder?"

Daisy touched the envelope. "If you open it, you will find out!"

Father Christmas opened the envelope. "I don't know how long the envelope has been here; it must have fallen out of my pocket onto the seat!"

Daisy stroked her hair. "It must have fallen down the side of the seat at some point!"

Father Christmas had bright eyes. "Yes, that is why I couldn't find it because it was hidden, it says that a person has been terrorising people by stealing their magical shoes from their feet in Wakefield!"

Daisy sounded puzzled. "That's odd, and it says her name is Julie, and she is five years old who has sent the letter!"

Father Christmas pointed at a flashing red button, speaking over the tannoy. "Elves, we have got a problem, the emergency red flashing warning button obviously means that trouble is occurring worldwide!"

Head elf Daisy giggles. "I think that it is a little bit comical when people form groups to try to investigate where the shoes have come from that mould to the children's feet well from our Shoe Magic shop, and I didn't think that orthopaedic shoes would help with my posture, but I stand corrected!"

Father Christmas smiled. "Yes, their faces are a picture when I look back at them on the camera outside of the Shoe Magic shop because they can't find it again and a clip of Dom the magic stealer in his green and black outfit outside of the secure glasshouse yesterday in Leeds was odd because he is locked up where he belongs, I guess that it must be old footage from before he was last locked up!"

Chapter Two

Low Christmas Spirit

An elf sounded distressed in Father Christmas's workshop speaking to Father Christmas. "That means more hard work and stress is needed that could cause me and my elf colleagues a headache to find out who is causing chaos, making our precious planet Earth low on Christmas spirit, meaning that children will be disappointed, because they would have no gifts under their Christmas tree, Christmas Eve to make them happy ever again if the sleigh doesn't have five white lights lit up making it fly!"

Father Christmas put his empty cup down on the table. "I am puzzled to find out how Dom got out of the glasshouse in Leeds. I went there in person so that I could see with my own eyes to make sure that Dom could not leave without being let out!"

An elf asked Father Christmas. "Will everything be okay? Because we have organised all of the presents ready for the sleigh, and we need all five white lights to glow well with one hundred percent power!"

Father Christmas nodded up and down. "Course it will be okay, please just carry on with operation Christmas!"

Daisy asked. "So, how exactly did Dom steal all of the

Christmas magic dust last time to try to destroy Christmas?"

Father Christmas played with his hands, explaining. "Dom slowed time down using some magic oil sent out automatically from his badge secretly with it undetected to store the magic dust inside of his Polaroid camera photo, different mobile phones and power banks that only Dom could have access to through his badge!"

Daisy sounded surprised. "That is so bad, and this is going to make a dip in mural, we need the mural restoring as soon as possible!"

Father Christmas scratched his head. "Yes, it is, and it is going unnoticed, and the missing hidden magic dust will travel all over the world, people were oblivious until their items went missing and their mobile phones started to work slowly because of the oil letting the dust flow inside filling any spare space available!"

Daisy suggested. "Maybe we could send our other head elves Karen and Poppy to different areas around the world to investigate with Isla who is already in Wakefield running and organising our Shoe Magic shop, what do you think?"

Father Christmas nodded up and down. "Yes, we are already losing power with the lights flashing on and off intermittently in the North Pole, this is not a good situation!"

Daisy stroked her hair. "We need to do something, but I am not sure what!"

Father Christmas sounded to be in deep thought and a little distracted and stressed. "I know that it is definitely nothing to do with the heavy snow falling down outside, because that is a normal extreme weather that we love here in the North Pole while my elves and I organise everything from checking the naughty and nice list, looking after the sleigh, making the toys, wrapping the presents and looking after the reindeers ready for Christmas Eve and many more things besides?"

Daisy put her hand on Father Christmas's shoulder to reassure him that everything would be okay. "So, do you think that it is a good idea to send Karen and Poppy down to Wakefield because you never answered my question?"

Father Christmas smirked. "Yes, I think that is a good idea, Karen and Poppy can take one of the red Ho, Ho, Ho phones with them so that they can keep in contact with us and I have just noticed the weather forecast for our Shoe Magic shop, unfortunately it is very windy in Wakefield because there is a storm forming, and snowmen have to go to the vegetable market to pick their nose!"

Daisy stroked her hand. "You are daft, Father Christmas

and I am just thinking, when a snowman is in a bad mood, he has a meltdown!"

Father Christmas smiled. "We are daft as a brush the both of us!"

Karen and Poppy used some magic dust to travel down to Wakefield.

In Wakefield, at Father Christmas's undercover magical shoe shop called Shoe Magic, an elf called Isla spoke. "It is nice to see you both again, I hope this is just a social visit!"

Karen and Poppy smiled at Isla, with Poppy speaking. "Have you noticed anything strange going on? Because the red button is flashing at the North Pole!"

Isla explained. "As you know, the door only opens up when a person is low on Christmas spirit to welcome the low-spirited person in the shop, the magical elves give away the shoes full of magic dust free of charge that spreads plenty of Christmas spirit as people walk making the shoes flash purple and white, in exchange of the recipients promise to wear them, until they need a new pair to spread the magic!"

Poppy randomly moved her eyes around. "Do the shoes still play the tune Jingle Bells at first?"

Isla nodded up and down. "Yes, they still play jingle bells as their new owners' unique chosen shoes are put onto people's feet!"

Karen raised her eyebrows. "I think it is really clever and a miracle how flashing lights that people enjoy looking at, they can save Christmas when people wear their shoes!"

Poppy explained. "I agree, and normally, every pair of flashing shoes powers Father Christmas's sleigh, and everything in the North Pole toy factory, but sadly we are struggling with power outages with the low volume of Christmas spirit causing us unexpected major problems!"

Chapter Three

Flashing Lights Shoes

Isla sounded concerned. "The comfortable, well-fitted, magic shoes that grow with your feet normally naturally powers the factory well with no hiccups, it always amazes me how the magic from each pair of shoes makes everything run as smooth as clockwork!"

Up at the North Pole, Father Christmas's head elf, Daisy, is very worried that the shoes are losing power that helps Father Christmas's red sleigh to fly, speaking. "My guess is that this has got something to do with the Christmas clock losing time!"

Father Christmas is feeling ecstatic for sending Karen and Poppy, his elf assistants, down to Wakefield using their precious magic dust to investigate why there is less Christmas spirit.

In Wakefield, Father Christmas's elf assistants, Karen and Poppy, try to work out why Father Christmas's red sleigh will not fly with the results of the dip in Christmas spirit with Poppy speaking. "Wow, it is windy here, we will solve this problem!"

Karen noticed that fewer children were wearing flashing lights shoe speaking to Poppy. "We have only got until Christmas Eve to sort this problem out; we need everyone wearing purple and white flashing shoes!"

Poppy pointed at Dom stealing a pair of shoes from a child who had just left the Shoe Magic shop. "I think that we have got the culprit causing chaos!"

Karen started to chase behind Dom, speaking loudly to Poppy a short distance away. "Dom the magic stealer has run into a house garden, and he has vanished! "

A lady appeared from a house into the garden, speaking

to Karen. "My dog is obsessed with chasing people on bikes, I am impressed how he can ride a bike, and I noticed a man vanish into the floor under my garden, with help from some kind of elf a moment ago, is that who you were chasing?"

Karen thanked the lady, saying yes, and inspected the area where Dom had last walked back to the Shoe Magic shop, muttering to herself. "I think that lady has just told me a dog joke and Dom has slipped away. I just do not know where he has gone or how he entered under the floor?"

Poppy raised her voice in disbelief. "We caught Dom red-handed. How did he get away so fast? This is a disappointing result, and I am just thinking, the other day a tree tried to run away, but it isn't out of the woods yet?"

Isla chuckled, suggesting. "Maybe Dom has got an associate helping him, what do you think?"

Karen sounded upset. "We need to go back to the garden where Dom and his elf disappeared to investigate the exact spot where they vanished into the ground!"

Poppy sounded puzzled. "What do you mean, Karen?"

Karen grabbed Isla and Poppy's hands. "Please just lock the Shoe Magic door and erect the force field, Isla, and come with me!"

Isla, Karen, and Poppy walked back to the garden and watched from a distance, with Isla speaking. "Wow, Dom has just appeared out of the garden with his small round badge flashing a light-yellow colour on his top!"

Karen had a puzzled look, pointing at an elf following behind Dom closing the floor up behind him with no trace of them doing anything. "I guess they must be using the magic that they have stolen somehow to cover the hole in the floor!"

Poppy suggested. "I think we need to start looking at people's cameras and phones in the secret settings mode to find out if our magic is stored inside that Dom has secretly put there magically using his oil!"

Isla scratched her ear while looking into space in deep thought. "We need to talk people into letting us look at their personal electronic items so that we can work out if they have been hacked by Dom!"

Poppy pointed. "Look, both of them have got a yellow badge on, I guess they could be storing all of the magic from the stolen shoes in their badges!"

Chapter Four

Ho, Ho, Ho Phone

Isla shouted to Dom and the elf. "Dom and your elf friend, please stop walking away!"

Dom shouted back. "No, because you are obviously after our yellow badges, and you will never get hold of them!"

Karen grabbed Dom's hand. "You are both coming with us to the Shoe Magic shop now!"

Father Christmas rang on the red HO, HO, HO phone with him speaking to Poppy. "How is it panning out in Wakefield? Have you got any further with your investigation?"

Poppy explained. "We have found Dom and one of your elves who is helping Dom!"

Father Christmas sounded more positive. "I will leave you to sort it out. You are doing an excellent job, and I am disappointed with my elf for being sneaky and unreliable. We will speak again soon!"

Poppy sounded proud. "We are doing our best!"

Father Christmas ended the call on the Ho, Ho, Ho phone having a moan. "We are running out of time because it is the end of November now!"

Isla turned off the force field with her gold magic key, deactivating it.

They all walked into the Shoe Magic shop with Karen speaking to Dom. "So, is it you and your elf friend that have been stealing our shoes from people because you couldn't get in because of the force field protecting it, and how did you escape from the glasshouse in Leeds?"

Dom replied, swerving the answer. Yes, I have been wanting to have a look around in this Shoe Magic shop. Can we please have a look around before you send us to the secure glasshouse?"

Karen had a stern tone of voice. "I will repeat my question; how did you escape from the secure glasshouse in Leeds in the United Kingdom?"

Dom had a sly grin on his face explaining. "I managed to

sneak out by some kind of miracle with help from my new elf friend Mateo and a good disguise, so I looked like a guard blending in well?"

Poppy breathed heavily, sounding indecisive. "So, you are a crafty person, Dom, and I do not know about that, it may be too risky to let you look around the Shoe Magic shop on your own because you are a sly piece of work, please give us your badges!"

Dom shook his head from side to side. "We can't because they are stuck to us and anyone that touches them, they will have a nasty shock to their body that could be life-threatening!"

Karen touched the elf's badge, getting a shock shaking. "We will get the badges off their clothes somehow; this has shaken me up a bit!"

The elf answered in a sarcastic tone. "Dom did warn you that you would be in danger, it isn't our fault that you didn't listen, and can we please look around the Shoe Magic shop?"

Isla replied. "I suppose you could have a little walk around as long as you promise not to touch anything, but only if it is okay with Poppy and Karen!"

Karen and Poppy agreed and organised transport for Dom and his elf friend to go to the glasshouse while Isla walked around with Dom and his elf, looking sheepish, with Dom asking a question, pointing at a large red vault. "Is that where you store the magic for the shoes that you make?"

Isla nodded up and down. "Yes, you will never have any more magical dust ever again that we put inside of the shoes that we give away for free to spread the magic of the Christmas spirit! "

Dom laughed. "You are wrong because me and my elf have got it all now because our yellow badges are invisibly pulling all of the dust inside of our badges like a vacuum as we speak and any excess magic dust that will not fit is travelling towards many victims' random local electronic devices nearby!"

Isla smirked. "You need to walk back to Karen and Poppy to get picked up now so that you can be taken back to the secure glasshouse where you belong!"

Isla, Dom, and Mateo walked back to Karen and Poppy.

Poppy was speaking with Father Christmas on the Ho, Ho, Ho phone, with Isla speaking. "We need to not let Dom and Mateo out of our sight because Dom and Mateo have got all of our magic from the Shoe Magic shop inside of their yellow badges and some random electrical devices!"

Chapter Five

Magic Stealer Eve

Father Christmas sounded upset. "I heard that. It is not sounding good; and I think the car has arrived. You need to not waste a second and get Dom and Mateo inside of the car immediately so they cannot get away!"

Father Christmas ended the Ho, Ho, Ho call.

Karen slapped her thigh in anger. "This situation gets worse, and at least the wind has slowed down a little bit, but it's still blowing well!"

Poppy sounded upset. "I wish I could have shared some better news with Father Christmas. The only good thing is, we have got hold of Dom and Mateo!"

They walked outside with the wind howling, with Dom and

Mateo running away as they were about to get into a large car with blackened windows.

Poppy shouted. "Come back, please!"

Dom shouted back, fighting against the wind, running as fast as he could, with Mateo slightly behind him, sounding evil, laughing as he spoke. "No chance, our plan worked, we have got what we wanted, more control of all of the magic, you will never see us again, instead of it being Christmas Eve, it will be Magic Stealer Eve with a lump of coal instead of a nicely wrapped gift for my lovely victims, I mean children from now on that will never believe in Father Christmas again, I have won, everyone will be in misery together, but it will be fun for me!"

Karen started to chase Dom and Mateo. "We will find you and stop you!"

Dom shouted back. "You wish. People will be able to pay a

high price for a nice gift and fun times, it will be like a jukebox, you put money in, and you get on the nice list or people would just get a gift back in exchange or a bit of entertainment, so it's not all bad!"

Dom and Mateo disappeared from sight.

Karen walked back to Poppy and Isla, with Isla sounding down speaking. "What do we do now because people need to believe in Father Christmas, not pay for the privilege to feel happy and experience joy?"

Poppy suggested to visit a local junior school to ask for their help speaking. "I think that we need to warn people about Dom and Mateo and plan a trap for them!"

Isla sounded disappointed. "I will carry on giving the Shoe Magic shop shoes out in the shop for nothing, while you both try to work out some kind of plan!"

Karen and Poppy agreed walking out of the Shoe Magic shop with Karen speaking. "We need to do a bit of investigating by going into this junior school, and we need to ask the children in the assembly how many of them have had their shoes stolen by Dom the magic stealer!"

Karen got an ID badge out of her pocket that would change to whatever authority was needed to get access to the school.

Poppy and Karen walked into the school and asked the receptionist if they could ask for the children's help, with Karen showing her ID badge with the receptionist agreeing. "Yes, with you being the government investigators team to gain the evidence needed for your task to work out which child is the brightest and will fit your intellectual quiz tournament in Wakefield, of course you can, please go through to the assembly, it is straight in front of you as you walk down the corridor!"

In the school assembly, Karen asked the children. "How many of you have had your shoes stolen?"

Nearly every hand was raised into the air with Poppy sighing, speaking. "Okay, thank you, children, we are going in a moment. Can anyone please tell me who stole your shoes and what the people or person looked like?"

Karen whispered to Poppy. "I think we are in deep trouble because nearly everyone has put their hands up, and they look upset with them probably remembering their shoes being stolen. Their magic-less shoes need to be swapped urgently to magical shoes!"

Poppy asked the children who did not have their shoes stolen to line up and have them scanned to make sure that they have got the full amount of magic dust inside of them, speaking. "Could we please check your phones as well to see if any hidden magic is inside of them, so that we can send it back up to the North Pole for Father Christmas and his elves to use because it is urgently needed and any magic dust can stay in your shoes!"

Many children moaned about their phones slowing down when they were trying to use them.

Poppy sounded deflated. "Sadly, that means that the majority of the phones around here have been hacked by Dom and Mateo, and the silver Christmas clock needs to get back to its full speed pronto!"

A young girl quizzed Poppy. "What does that mean?"

Poppy hesitated to speak with Karen muttering. "It unfortunately means that Dom and Mateo are out of control, and they are in charge of Christmas,

and it will never be the same
again!"

The girl wiped a tear from
her eye. "So, that explains why
the grotto is not there this year!"

Karen nodded up and down.
"Yes, sorry about that!"

The young girl walked off full
of disappointment with her head
down sniffling wiping her eyes.

Chapter Six

Christmas Bank Scanner

Only four people got in the queue, with Karen's face dropping speaking. "This is so sad because that means that most of our shoes have been stolen, I am scared that Christmas will never happen ever again as we know it right now at this rate!"

A male child started to cry, speaking. "You are trying your best, I can see, but I could not imagine having no presents on Christmas Eve, so that we can play with them on Christmas Day, this is making me feel sad!"

Poppy hugged the male child, speaking. "Don't worry, we are determined to mend this awkward hard-to-solve puzzle!"

Karen nodded. "Yes, we will work out what we need to do to

correct the wrong, please don't panic, I know that it is hard not to!"

Poppy scanned each shoe that contained magic dust, with them all needing extra magic dust speaking. "You will all get invited into our Shoe Magic shop by Isla as you walk past!"

Karen scanned each phone using the Christmas bank scanner speaking. "Well, so far, some phones have got magical dust inside of them. I have sent the dust available back up to the North Pole through the Christmas bank scanner from the phones!"

Suddenly the Ho, Ho, Ho phone rang with Father Christmas explaining to Karen speaking. "Our friend the Easter Bunny may know where Dom and his elf are, and the power isn't going out as much, have you sent some magic dust back to us?"

Everyone dropped silent, listening to their conversation.

Karen sounded more positive. "Yes, we have sent some magic dust up to the North Pole from some phones, I cannot say that it will be loads, but it will help a bit, and I am pleased that the wind has died down a bit more!"

Father Christmas sounded down. "Please put all of your efforts into finding Dom and Mateo. We urgently need the magic from their badges back!"

Karen sighed. "We are doing everything that we can. Our Christmas elves play such a massive part in clawing back the magical dust, putting it back where it belongs so that Father Christmas's sleigh will fly, and where can we find the Easter Bunny?"

Father Christmas raised his voice slightly. "You need to find the large Easter eggs along the pavement, that is your trail like breadcrumbs to find him!"

Everyone agreed to help to find the Easter eggs, with Karen putting the Ho, Ho, Ho phone down to Father Christmas, ending the call.

Poppy explained to the children. "Please do not worry. If you know someone who has got a special pair of shoes from us, please make sure that they do not walk alone because they will be stolen by Dom the magic stealer and Mateo if they are alone!"

They then thanked the
children and walked out of the
junior school.

Karen explained to Poppy
that the Easter Bunny has got an
idea where to find Dom. With
Poppy noticing large milk
chocolate Easter eggs along the
pavement, they then noticed the
Easter Bunny as they were
walking away from the junior
school with Poppy shouting him.
"Easter Bunny, Father Christmas
mentioned that you can help to

find Dom and Mateo, is this true?"

Karen complimented the Easter Bunny. "Your fur looks lovely and fluffy white; you groom up well. I am sorry for interrupting and stalling your answer!"

The Easter Bunny nodded up and down looking a little startled in his face. "I do try, and Dom the magic stealer keeps moving to different places. That garden is where he was last seen, but I have found Dom and Mateo again!"

Poppy sounded grateful. "I think we are hopefully on the right track!"

Karen asked the Easter Bunny where Dom was. "Do you know where Dom and Mateo are? Please take us there if you do!"

They walked for five minutes down a busy road full of traffic, pedestrians, and many shops with the Easter Bunny pushing a large fluffy white trolley containing a large yellow square box that is called an Easter egg caster with him speaking. "Don't worry, we don't have far to go, I will turn my trolley into my fluffy white trolley car using my yellow button so that we can travel there faster!"

The Easter Bunny, Karen and Poppy got into the car, with Poppy speaking. "Are we nearly there and how does the Easter egg caster work?"

The Easter Bunny winked. "It is my special magical hands that are my secret thing making things happen for people in need!"

They arrived at their destination after a few minutes and left the car with the Easter Bunny pressing a yellow button to turn it back into a trolley.

Chapter Seven

Easter Egg Maker

The Easter Bunny pointed at a large flower. "Dom and Mateo have entered inside of the middle of that flower, and I have put a magical trap on them using my Easter egg caster that produces an A4 size of chocolate paper that expands into any size Easter egg that I choose using different buttons to pour different amounts of chocolate as needed for the thickness of the egg into it!"

Poppy sounded amazed. "That is so clever!"

The Easter Bunny carried on explaining. "It is good yes, and if they leave the flower, they will get trapped inside of that large milk chocolate Easter egg at the side of the flower because my chocolate sucker that is built inside of the egg, it grows naturally inside of the egg that will suck Dom and Mateo inside of the middle of the chocolate egg!"

Karen organised a car to transport Mateo and Dom to the secure glasshouse in Leeds speaking. "I just hope that they do not come out of the flower before the transport arrives, in case they break themselves out of the chocolate!"

Poppy ran to a local shop, grabbing hold of a large black net that was for sale in a fishing shop, with her running back to

Karen and the Easter Bunny, speaking. "I will put this over the flower so that they will be hopefully trapped or, if that fails, they will get trapped and encased in the Easter egg by the chocolate sucker that is inside of the egg, making a sticky mess!"

The shopkeeper ran behind Poppy asking for payment for the net. "You have not paid for the net; can you please pay now?"

The Easter Bunny used his Easter egg maker from his trolley

that looked a bit larger than a shopping trolley on wheels that pushed properly. "There you go, I have made the egg in my trolley, don't eat the chocolate egg all at once!"

The shopkeeper thanked the Easter Bunny for the chocolate egg, walking away licking his lips, muttering loudly. "That was amazing how the chocolate expanded automatically into a chocolate egg, that was well worth watching

and this looks so deliciously
yummy!"

Karen pointed at a large
black car that had arrived for
Dom and Mateo with Karen
speaking. "I just hope that they
come out of the flower soon!"

Dom and Mateo appeared
out of the flower getting tangled
in the fishing net, with the car
driver, Karen, Poppy, and the
Easter Bunny pulling Dom and
Mateo into the car with Dom and
Mateo getting trapped inside of

the Easter egg with the egg pulling them inside, Karen shouted to them. "I hope that you are allergic to chocolate because you are both staying inside of the Easter egg until you arrive at the secure glasshouse, and it will serve you right if anything bad happens to you!"

Dom threatened. "Me and elf Mateo will lick or bite our way out of our Easter egg. It feels like I am suffocating in here, and I hate not being able to see!"

Karen grinned. "I am just thinking, tell someone who is bothered, and if you do get out of the Easter egg, the fishing net has tangled you into a organised mess like you are handcuffed together and you will be carried out of the car being extremely sick due to an overload of chocolate, and I learnt at school that the word clock in Spanish is reloj!

Poppy sounded impressed with Karen's knowledge agreeing, then rang Father Christmas on the Ho, Ho, Ho phone. "Hello Father Christmas, Karen is clever knowing some Spanish and Dom and Mateo are on their way to the secure glasshouse in Leeds as we speak. I just thought that I would let you know, and I heard on the grapevine that they only sell plain chocolate at the airport!"

Father Christmas sounded extremely happy, chuckling. "I like your chocolate joke with it being in the airport, and thank goodness for that, I am proud of you all for saving Christmas.

Christmas will hopefully officially happen this year with no more hiccups along the way and many smiling faces will show their happiness!"

Poppy ended the Ho, Ho, Ho call and spoke. "You are getting locked up where you belong, both of you, you are a pair of idiots, I thought that you would have learnt your lesson from when you attempted this Christmas robbery previously!"

The Easter Bunny, Poppy and Karen used the Easter Bunny's fluffy white trolley car to follow behind Dom and Mateo.

After an hour of driving, they arrived at the secure glasshouse in Leeds, with Dom and Mateo covered in melted chocolate dripping from them, and they were fully surrounded by soldiers, with Dom speaking. "You can not lock us up!"

Glasshouse soldiers dressed in black and dark blue

held a large glass empty vacuum pipe up towards Dom and Mateo's milk chocolate badges with the vacuums being filled with magic dust from their badges, with Dom and Mateo attempting to run away with Dom shouting. "You can't do this; we collected that magic dust in our badges through hard work, and all we can do is slide about underfoot with the stickiness of the chocolate making it slippery!"

Karen, the Easter Bunny, and Poppy watched Dom and

Mateo trying to sneak away unsuccessfully with them falling over their feet. Dom and Mateo walked into the glasshouse down the steps from the court as fast as a domino being rushed by the guards, with Mateo sounding threatening, shouting. "We will get out again at some point, don't you worry!"

The red Ho, Ho, Ho phone rang, with Poppy answering with an excited Father Christmas sounding happy. "Our elves have received all of the magic dust, and the silver Christmas clock is running back at the normal speed again, and it is Christmas Eve already!"

Poppy screamed with excitement. "We did it between us as a team achieving our goal that we needed to replace all of the Christmas spirit to save Christmas, please get the red sleigh ready, we are on our way back up to the North Pole in the next twenty minutes using our magic dust!"

The Easter Bunny jollily hopped away pushing his trolley, speaking. "I am going back to join my bunny friends to organise and make my chocolate eggs for Easter. I am glad that I could help. See you soon!"

Father Christmas squealed with joy. "Thank you, Easter Bunny, you helped to save Christmas and our sleigh is ready to go any second because the elves have put full effort into stocking it, and all five white lights are finally showing up on the red sleigh, all of our children and adults that we visit will be so excited in the morning to open their presents with most of them unaware of our problems that we have solved, I think that is a massive achievement!"

Poppy gave the Ho, Ho, Ho phone to Isla. "You deserve a reward letter for all of your hard work!"

Isla wiped a tear from her eye. "It is a pleasure to help to save Christmas, you're more than welcome!"

Father Christmas apologised, saying that he had to go and put the Ho, Ho, Ho phone down. "I am sorry, but I am going to have to put the phone down so that I can thank my elves here in the North Pole in person for their hard work and cheer myself up using my special telescope that looks at Christmas trees and the most decorated houses near and far to award someone with the most decorated home!"

Isla glowed with happiness.
"Ok Father Christmas, it was
lovely speaking with you, bye for
now!"

They put the Ho, Ho, Ho
phone down.

Isla got an official thank-you
letter from Father Christmas for
being loyal.

Poppy and Karen used
some magic dust to reappear

back at the side of Father Christmas in the North Pole.

Father Christmas and his elves organised Christmas and left Dom and Mateo a lump of coal each with the guards so they could pass it on to them, saying that is all that they deserved.

Father Christmas landed on a certain roof, clattering loudly with him flowing down the chimney, and he entered into the fireplace with a little girl waking up on the sofa speaking. "Hello

Father Christmas, I see that my letter worked because you have made more magical shoes to spread the magic well and you have left a trail of magical dust behind you making the star at the top of our Christmas tree glow!"

Father Christmas put Julie's Christmas present under the Christmas tree and spoke. "Yes, your letter made a difference. Christmas will always be magical for everyone from now on!"

Julie thanked Father Christmas. "I am looking forward to opening my gift in the morning with my parents. I will go back to sleep now, thank you so much!"

Father Christmas looked emotional, nodding up and down, wiping a tear of joy from his cheek. "You're welcome. I know that you will love your gift. You deserve your present for staying on the good list!"

Father Christmas returned to his sleigh and landed on every

roof a little more gently so that he did not wake any more children.

Julie opened her gift with her parents on Christmas Day morning; and she loved her new baby doll.

Father Christmas rewarded a lucky family in Wakefield, West Yorkshire in the United Kingdom for the best decorations in the entire world with a lifetime of visits from the reindeer's every Christmas, so long as they still decorate their house, or the reward would move onto the next best decorated home.

Karen and Poppy helped to prepare the year aheads toys for every child in the world.

Every child in the world had more than enough Christmas spirit to power the sleigh and everything in the North Pole.

The mural is fully restored with everybody working as a team to get everything done to a good standard, making everyone

feel ecstatically happier with
more than enough get up and go.

The End.

Other books by the author Anita Kirk

About the author

Anita Kirk is from Yorkshire in the United Kingdom, she works full time and writes many book genres in her spare time with unlimited talent to write anything, she loves swimming, line dancing, holidays, music, films, writing, reading, and spending time with friends and family.

All of Anita Kirk's books have got <u>funny moments</u> that may make you feel like laughing your socks off.

These books have been written so far with many more available soon.

PLEASE TYPE ANITA KIRK INTO AMAZON

FOR ALL AVAILABLE PUBLISHED BOOKS

OF MANY DIFFERENT GENRES.

Remember that you can follow and contact Anita Kirk with any questions or comments on Tick Tock, Facebook, Twitter, LinkedIn or you can email any comments to anitajane1@outlook.com
Please contact Anita if you would like a shop opening or anything else and she will get back to you as soon as possible with an answer.
If you have enjoyed reading Anita Kirk's books a

good review would be appreciated and if you could share Anita's books on your social media, and with your family and friends she would really appreciate your help.
Thank you for your support in reading this book.
All of Anita Kirk's books are available on Amazon and some other online shops.

A good review would mean a lot if you have enjoyed this book.
Thank you in advance for your good positive review it is very much appreciated.

__Erotically Spooky__ is the same as __Spooky Scary__ but it has got a little bit of raunch, and vampires attempt to take over the world with funny moments to make you laugh out loud.

__Thank you.__

Anita Kirk, author

@AnitaKi73550337

Twitter –

Author Anita Kirk

LinkedIn-

Instagram-

@anitakirkauthor

You can also follow Anita Kirk on tick tock.

www.ingramcontent.com/pod-product-compliance
Lightning Source LLC
Chambersburg PA
CBHW060436130626
46555CB00005B/2387